Saving Mr Hoot

Helen Stephens

There was an owl in the tree
outside Ben's house. Every night,
Ben called to him,

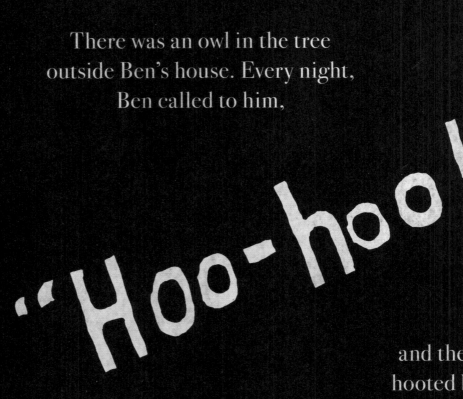

"Hoo-hoo!"

and the owl
hooted back,

"Hoo-
hoo-
hoo!"

Ben called him
Mr Hoot.

But no one else seemed to notice Mr Hoot. Perhaps that's because owls are wild animals. They just don't do what you want them to.

So when Ben said to his dad, "Look! There he is!"

Mr Hoot hid in his nest hole and Dad couldn't see him.

And when Mr Hoot
swooped down and stole
his oaty biscuit, only
Ben saw him.

"I *have* to have another one,"
said Ben. "Mr Hoot took mine."

Mum didn't look like she believed
him. (But she let him have another
biscuit just the same.)

One evening, Ben was waving
to Mr Hoot when the owl swished
down and swiped the fluffy mitten
right off Ben's hand.

"Where's your other glove?" asked Dad.
"Mr Hoot took it!" said Ben.
Dad didn't look like he
believed him, either.

That night, Ben told Mr Hoot,
"You're getting me into trouble!"
"Hoo-hoo-hoo!" said Mr Hoot.
It sounded like he was laughing.

Then Mr Hoot swooshed back up to his nest in the old beech tree.

Ben imagined him snuggled up with his fluffy mitten.

All winter long, Ben and Mr Hoot called to each other.

Then, in springtime, Ben
saw a notice by Mr Hoot's tree.
"What does 'Tree Felling' mean?"
he asked his mum.

TREE
FELLING

"Oh, it's so sad," said Mum.
"They're chopping that old tree down."
Ben couldn't believe it. That was Mr Hoot's home!
Grown-ups were very strange.

That night, Ben didn't want a bedtime story. He was too worried.
"Where will Mr Hoot live if they cut down his tree?"

Mum smiled. "He's not a real owl, is he?
Nobody sees him but you."
"He *is* real!" shouted Ben. "I'll show you!"
He ran to the window and called:

"Hoo-hoo-hoooo!"

But there was no reply.
"He must be out," said Ben, sadly.
"Come on," said Mum.
"Bedtime."

But Ben couldn't sleep.

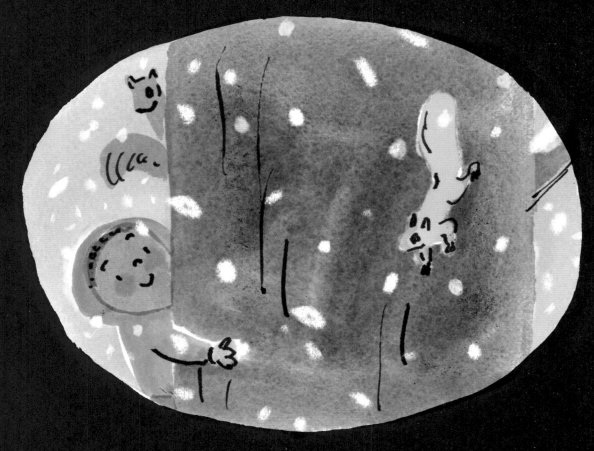

The old beech tree wasn't
just Mr Hoot's house.

All sorts of creatures lived in it.

Where would they all go?

Next morning,
Ben woke up to a
terrible noise.

There was a lady outside
by the tree – and she had a
huge chainsaw!

Ben raced to the door.
"Come on, Mum and Dad!
There's no time to lose!"

"STOP!"

cried Ben.

"You can't chop this tree down," said Ben. "It's Mr Hoot's home!"
The chainsaw lady looked very surprised. So did all the
neighbours who'd come out to watch.

"Who's Mr Hoot?"
said everyone.

"He's an owl," said Ben. "And he lives in this tree,
and he's probably hiding because he's frightened.
Come back tonight and you'll see him. I promise."

That night they all camped out under the tree.
"Listen!" said Ben, and he called:

"Hoo-hoo-hooooo!"

There was no reply.
The children giggled.

Ben called again:

"Hoo-hoo-hooooo!"

Still no reply.
"Hee-hee-hee!" giggled
the children.

"Shhh!" said Ben.
He tried one last time . . .

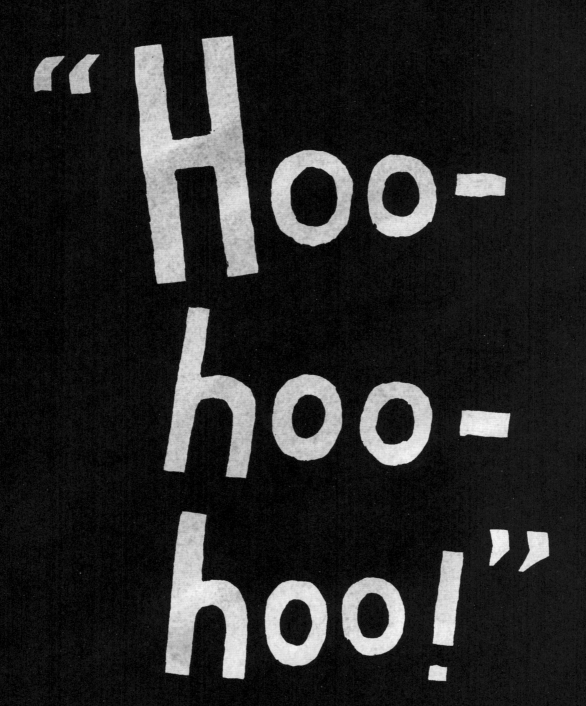

"Hoo-
hoo-
hoo!"

There was a long silence, then . . .

hoooo!"

called Mr Hoot.

Everyone gasped.
"You were right, Ben! There *is* an owl!"
"Oh, no, there isn't!" said Ben.
He looked through his dad's binoculars.

"There are TWO owls . . .

... and THREE eggs!"

And a few weeks later . . .

. . . there were two big Hoots, and three little Hoots, living in the tree that Ben saved.

I've always loved owls – I drew this one
when I was just eight years old.

Saving Mr Hoot was inspired by an owl who lived
in some lovely big old trees on my street. I used
to love hearing him hooting at night. Sadly some
grown-ups chopped down the trees, so that they
could put up brighter street lights. After that,
I never saw my owl again. Those bright lights
must have frightened him away.

This book is dedicated to that owl, and to
all the wildlife that lives in our towns.

Helen Stephens

First published in 2021 by Alison Green Books
An imprint of Scholastic
Euston House, 24 Eversholt Street, London NW1 1DB
Scholastic Ireland, 89E Lagan Road,
Dublin Industrial Estate, Glasnevin, Dublin D11 HP5F
www.scholastic.co.uk
Designed by Zoë Tucker

Text and illustrations copyright © 2021 Helen Stephens

ISBN HB: 978 1 407191 96 6
ISBN PB: 978 1 407191 97 3

FSC
www.fsc.org

MIX
Paper from
responsible sources
FSC® C008047